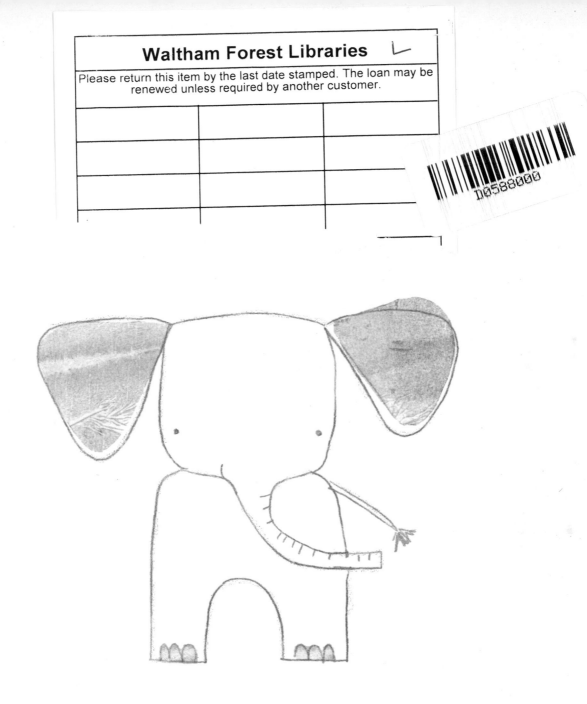

Small Elephant's Bathtime

by **Tatyana Feeney**

OXFORD
UNIVERSITY PRESS

Small Elephant **loved** water.

He **loved** jumping in puddles.

He **loved** to drink water
through his curly red straw.

But he did **not** love water...

when it was
in a bath.

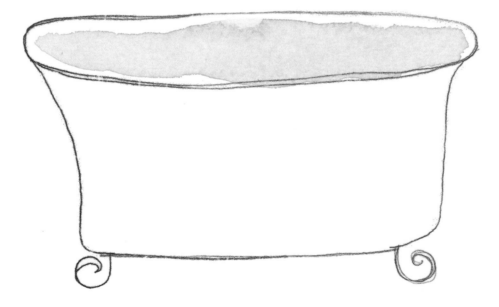

Small Elephant's Mummy tried to make his bath more exciting.

She tried all sorts of toys.

But Small Elephant
was not interested.

She tried blowing bubbles.

But Small Elephant
was not fooled.

**And, as bathtime got closer,
Small Elephant got busier.**

**'I'm too
busy
playing!'**

Small Elephant
got crosser.

'No!'

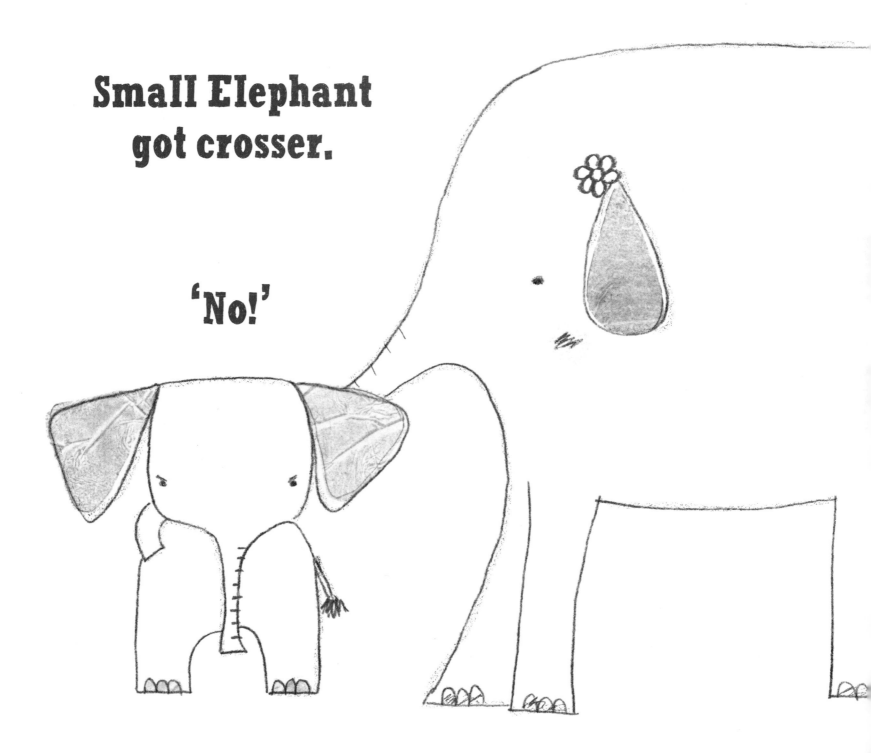

And crosser, and crosser,
and crosser.

'No.'

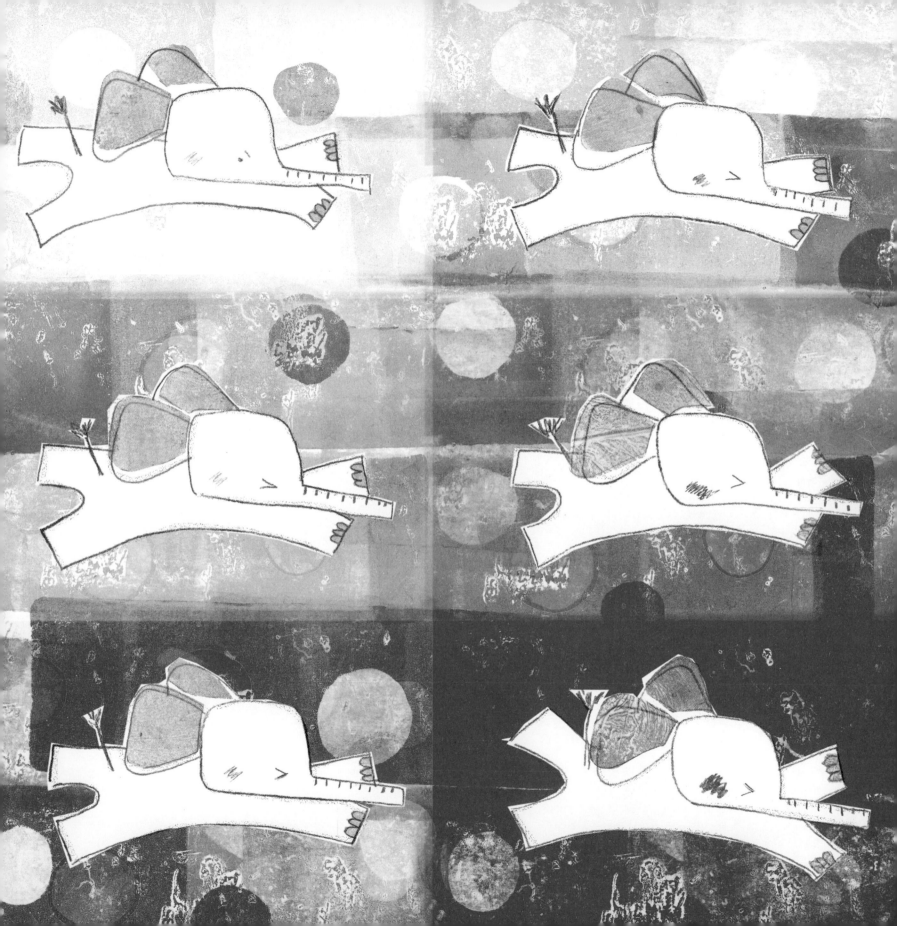

**Then Small Elephant
got harder to find.**

There was only
one more thing
for Mummy
to try.

Daddy!

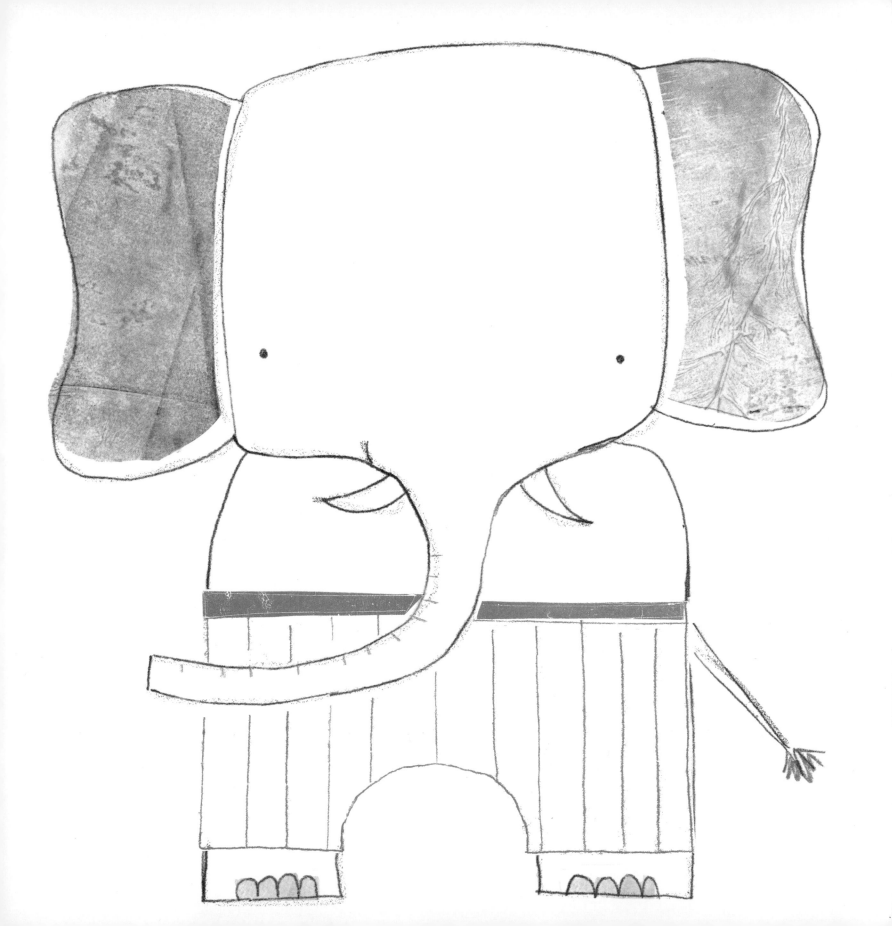

Daddy was **too** **big** for the bath.

Daddy looked **very** **silly** in the bath.

Small Elephant started to giggle.

'Hey!' he laughed.
'That's **my** bath.'

Daddy was happy to get out of the bath.

**And Small Elephant
was happy to get in.**

And he was **even happier** to stay in.

So, when Mummy said it was time to get out,

Small Elephant said . . .

To Juliet – a little mermaid who always loves her bath

OXFORD
UNIVERSITY PRESS

Great Clarendon Street, Oxford OX2 6DP

Oxford University Press is a department of the University of Oxford.
It furthers the University's objective of excellence in research, scholarship,
and education by publishing worldwide in

Oxford   New York

Auckland   Cape Town   Dar es Salaam   Hong Kong   Karachi
Kuala Lumpur   Madrid   Melbourne   Mexico City   Nairobi
New Delhi   Shanghai   Taipei   Toronto

With offices in

Argentina   Austria   Brazil   Chile   Czech Republic   France   Greece
Guatemala   Hungary   Italy   Japan   Poland   Portugal   Singapore
South Korea   Switzerland   Thailand   Turkey   Ukraine   Vietnam

Oxford is a registered trade mark of Oxford University Press
in the UK and in certain other countries

Text and illustrations © Tatyana Feeney 2015

British Library Cataloguing in Publication Data available

ISBN: 978-0-19-273737-3 (hardback)
ISBN: 978-0-19-273738-0 (paperback)

2 4 6 8 10 9 7 5 3 1

Printed in China

Paper used in the production of this book is a natural,
recyclable product made from wood grown in sustainable forests.
The manufacturing process conforms to the environmental
regulations of the country of origin

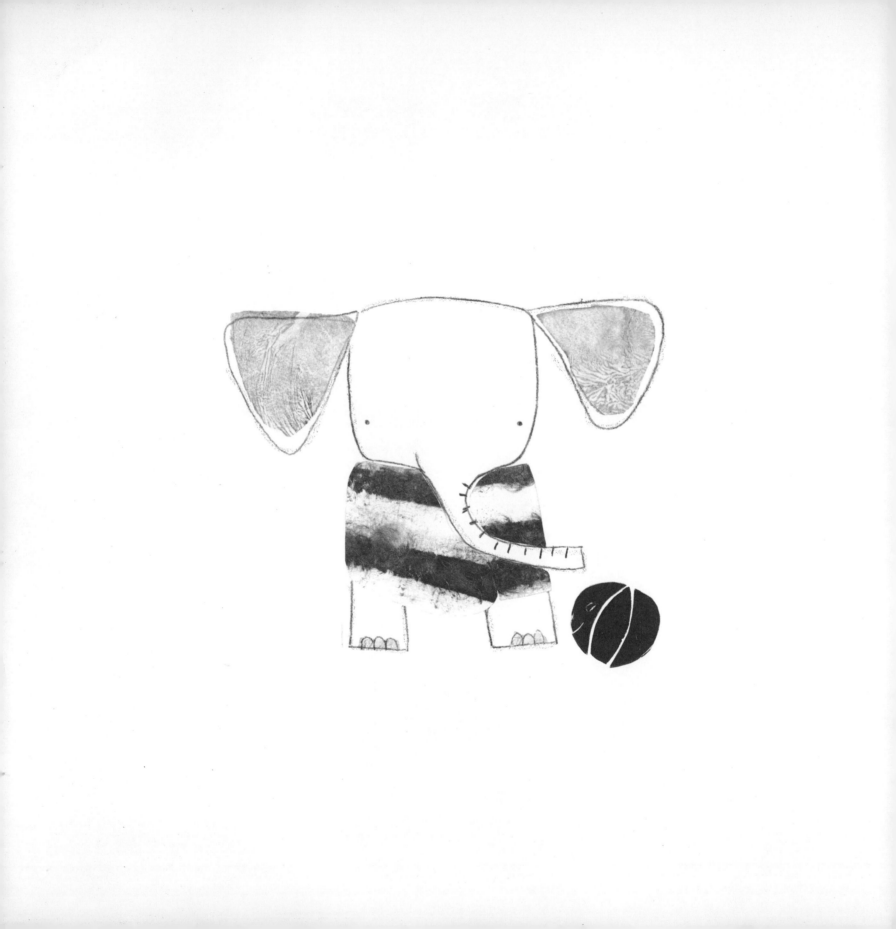